LET'S WORK IT OUT™

How to deal with ANGER

Julie Fiedler

PowerKiDS press.

New York

Published in 2007 by The Rosen Publishing Group, Inc.
29 East 21st Street, New York, NY 10010

First Edition

Editor: Jennifer Way
Book Design: Ginny Chu
Layout Design: Kate Laczynski
Photo Researcher: Sam Cha

Photo Credits: Cover, pp. 1, 12 © Elaine Duigenan/Getty Images; p. 4 image copyright Jerry Bernard, 2006. Used under license from Shutterstock, Inc.; p. 18 © Corbis; pp. 6, 8, 10, 14, 16, 20 © superstock.com.

Library of Congress Cataloging-in-Publication Data

Fiedler, Julie.
   How to deal with anger / Julie Fiedler. — 1st ed.
       p. cm. — (Let's work it out)
   Includes index.
   ISBN-13: 978-1-4042-3671-4 (library binding)
   ISBN-10: 1-4042-3671-6 (library binding)
   1. Anger—Juvenile literature. I. Title.
   BF575.A5F54 2007
   152.4'7—dc22
                                                2006026278

Manufactured in the United States of America
CPSIA Compliance Information: Batch #WRW902090PK: For Further Information contact Rosen Publishing, New York, New York at 1-800-237-9932

Contents

Everyone has different things that make them angry. It is important to find a way to deal with anger that works for you.

Everyone Gets Angry

Do you feel happiness? Sadness? Anger? These are all **emotions** that everyone feels. Certain emotions, such as anger, can be scary because they can be hard to control.

Anger can make people say or do hurtful things they do not mean. You can learn how to deal with anger in a healthy way. This will make you feel better and help keep your anger from controlling you. The first step is to understand what makes you angry and why.

Understanding what makes you angry is an important first step in dealing with anger.

Why Are You Angry?

Different **situations** can make you feel angry. If someone makes fun of you, that can make you angry. Other emotions, such as **jealousy** or **frustration**, can build up to anger. If you do not understand your homework, you might feel frustrated. Maybe a friend of yours has a toy you really want and you feel jealous.

What other situations can you think of that might make you angry? When you understand your anger, it will help you **express** yourself.

Talking to a parent is a good way to express your feelings.

Expressing Your Feelings

You can learn to **identify** feelings. This will help you express yourself in a healthy way. When you are angry, you might frown, get **tense**, or yell. These things can make you feel **stressed**, which can make you feel worse.

Expressing yourself can help you let go of the stress of anger if you do it in a safe way. One way to express yourself is to talk to your friends, family, teachers, or a trusted adult.

The stress from anger can give you a headache.

Don't Ignore Anger!

Anger can be stressful and scary, but if you **ignore** it, you will feel worse. You might feel the anger in your body. For example, you might feel so angry that you get a headache or stomachache.

If you ignore your anger for a long time, it might come out of you in other ways. You may hurt yourself, become sad, overeat, or pick fights. Your anger can get so bad that you might lose control. Anger can be **dangerous** if you keep it inside or let it out in unhealthy ways.

You might feel like yelling or destroying things when you are angry. This will not fix the problem that made you angry.

Unhealthy Ways to Deal with Anger

Dealing with your anger in unhealthy ways can be just as dangerous as not dealing with it at all. When people are angry, they may do things that are harmful to themselves or other people. People may say mean things, fight, seek **revenge**, or destroy things. Some people might drink or do drugs, which are very dangerous.

None of these things fixes the situation that made the person angry. They can often make things worse. This is why it is important to learn to handle your anger in a healthy way.

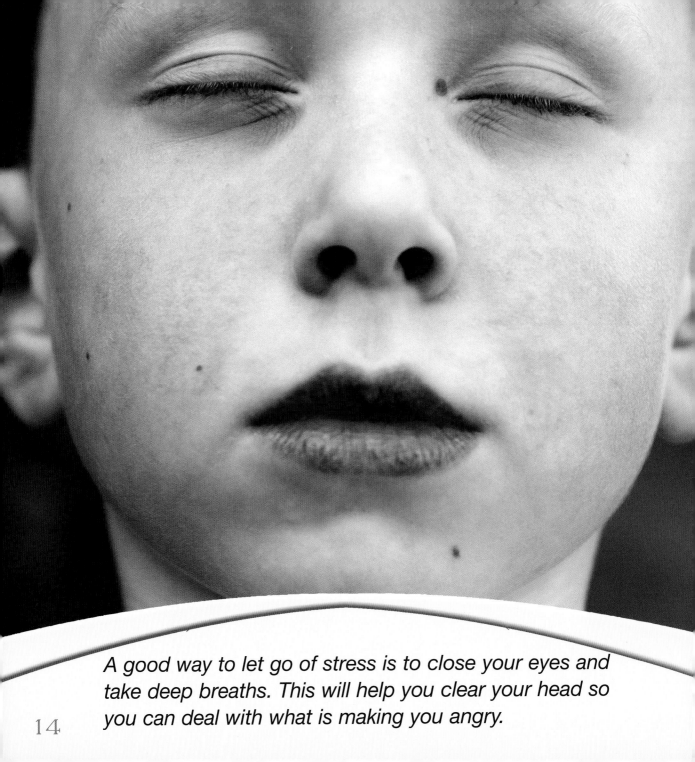

A good way to let go of stress is to close your eyes and take deep breaths. This will help you clear your head so you can deal with what is making you angry.

Handling Your Anger

What can you do when you are angry? The first thing is to try to let go of stress. Take deep breaths. Count to 10. Slow down. Instead of thinking about how angry you are, think positive thoughts. When you feel better, you can try to think through your problems.

Why are you angry? If you know what makes you mad, you can stay away from it or learn to deal with it. Calming down and thinking about why you are angry is the first step in dealing with your anger in a helpful way.

Talking to a trusted adult is a good way to deal with your feelings. He or she can help you find positive ways to work through your problem.

Talking It Out

Another thing you can do is talk about your anger to a parent, friend, teacher, or trusted adult. If you are angry with someone, you can talk to him or her when you are both calm.

When you talk about anger, talk about yourself and your feelings. Start your sentences with "I feel" and explain why you feel mad. Do not try to blame the other person. When you calmly talk about your feelings, you will feel better.

Making art, such as a painting, is one positive way to express your feelings.

Letting It Out

Sometimes you need to let anger out in other ways. **Exercise**, such as running or dancing, can help you let out angry tension. You can also write about your anger. If you cannot put your anger into words, draw a picture of how you feel or even of who made you mad.

These are all positive ways for you to express your anger. They will help you feel less tense and you can deal with your feelings.

Being around people who are angry can be stressful and scary.

When Other People Are Angry

It is OK to feel upset, or hurt, when other people are angry. Talk to them about how you feel. For example, say "I get upset when you yell because it scares me." It can be hard to express your feelings, but it will help people understand how their anger hurts others.

Anger can be **explosive**. If you ever feel in danger, get to a safe place and ask someone you trust for help. You can also get **professional** help when anger gets out of control.

Knowing How to Deal

Anger is one of many feelings. It is OK to feel anger from time to time. As you practice the things you learned in this book, you will learn to deal with anger and other emotions better. You can stop yourself before your anger gets out of control.

You will also set a good example for others in dealing with their anger. You will have learned a lot about dealing with anger in a healthy way.

Glossary

dangerous (DAYN-jeh-rus) Might cause hurt.

emotions (ih-MOH-shunz) Strong feelings.

exercise (EK-ser-syz) Things that are done to get or stay fit.

explosive (ek-SPLOH-siv) Something that can blow up.

express (ik-SPRES) To let out feelings.

frustration (frus-TRAY-shun) An upset feeling when one has trouble doing something.

identify (eye-DEN-tuh-fy) To tell what something is.

ignore (ig-NOR) To pay no attention to something.

jealousy (JEH-lus-ee) Wanting what someone else has.

professional (pruh-FESH-nul) Someone who is paid for what he or she does.

revenge (rih-VENJ) Hurting someone in return for hurting you.

situations (sih-choo-AY-shunz) Problems or things that happen.

stressed (STREST) Worried.

tense (TENS) Tight.

Index

Web Sites

Due to the changing nature of Internet links, PowerKids Press has developed an online list of Web sites related to the subject of this book. This site is updated regularly. Please use this link to access the list:
www.powerkidslinks.com/lwio/anger/